Pip and

Pip has a cap on.

Pip has a bat.

It is a big bat.

Pip can not hit it.

Pip has a big pan.

Pip can hit it.

Game page

On the next page is a game to help you practise reading the words in this book.

Photocopy the page 2, 3 or 4 times (depending on the number of players) onto card.

Cut the cards out and play snap.